LASERS

5.95

D0570271

Lynn Myring and Maurice Kimmitt

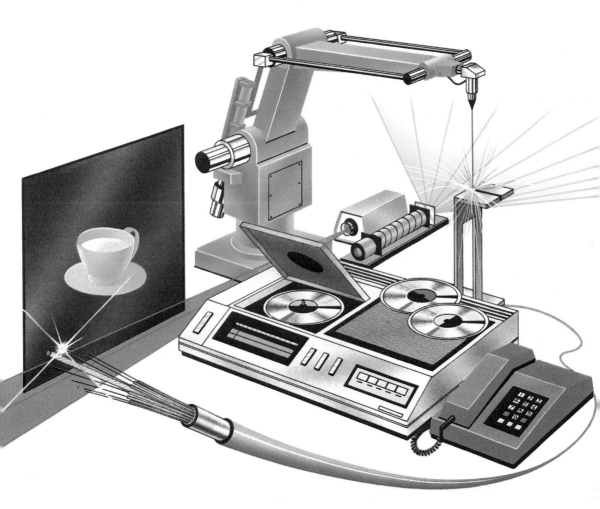

Assistant editor   Tony Potter

Designed by   Richard Lee, Roger Boffey, Roger Priddy, Gerry Downes

Illustrated by   Chris Lyon, Martin Newton,
Jeremy Gower, Simon Roulstone, Kai Choi,
Hussein Hussein, Graham Round

Contents

First published in 1984
by Usborne Publishing Ltd, 20 Garrick Street, London WC2 9BJ

Copyright © 1984 Usborne Publishing Ltd

All rights reserved. No part of this publication may be reproduced, stored in any form or by any means mechanical, electronic, photocopying, recording, or otherwise without the prior permission of the publisher.

About lasers

This book explains what lasers are and how they work, looking at the different kinds and showing how they are used. A laser is a device which produces beams of a special kind of light – laser light. A laser beam looks like a straight, almost solid, yet transparent rod of intense light. It is just light, but is quite

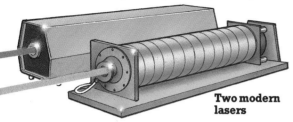

Two modern lasers

different from ordinary light in several ways, which are outlined on this page and explained later in this book.

A laser beam is light of only one colour; ordinary "white" light is many colours mixed together. Ordinary light spreads out in all directions; laser beams stay almost parallel. The lightwaves in a laser beam are in step with each other and work together to make the beam concentrated and very bright; ordinary light waves are not in step. In fact laser light is the brightest, most intense light known – even brighter than the sun.

The first laser

The theory of laser light was first suggested in 1957 by two American scientists, Charles Townes and Arthur Schawlow, but the first laser was not actually made until 1960. It was built by another American scientist, Theodore Maiman. This first laser was made from a rod of synthetic ruby and it created a laser beam when an intense flash of ordinary light was shone on it. Later research has shown that many materials, not just ruby, can be made to give off laser light – and that they can be stimulated in other ways as well as by light. Many different kinds of laser have been built and new kinds are being tried all the time. They all produce slightly different beams and so are useful for many varied jobs.

In its early days the laser was described as a solution looking for a problem. Scientists knew that it had many useful properties – beams were powerful enough to melt metals, yet could be focused to precise points for delicate work.

Now there are many thousands of problems which lasers are helping to solve. Lasers are used to cut, weld, engrave and make all kinds of things, from cars to clothing, from microchips to newspapers. Beams help build vertical skyscrapers and align underground pipes; they measure distances both microscopic and vast.

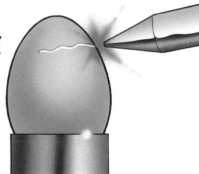

Laser delicately cutting eggshell

Lasers also carry phone calls and TV pictures over long distances, play video discs and scan bar codes in supermarkets. Doctors also use lasers for "bloodless surgery" which is less painful for the patient and easier for the surgeon. The laser has often proved to be better than traditional methods in all of these jobs, and many more. The development of the laser also gave scientists and artists the tool they needed to make amazing 3D photographs called holograms. The beams themselves are so beautiful that they are even used for special light shows and in concerts and discos.

Some everyday things processed by laser beams

Light and laser light

A laser produces light, but it is organized in a different way to the ordinary light of lamps and the Sun. Laser beams are different in several ways and it is these differences which make them special and useful for so many jobs.

These two pages look at both laser and ordinary light, explaining what they are and illustrating their differences and similarities.

Light waves

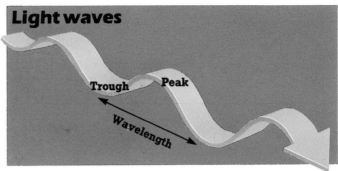

Light travels as a continuous stream of waves. The high points of a wave are called peaks, the low points troughs. Light is measured in two ways: by wavelength (the distance between two peaks) and by frequency (the number of waves a second).

Colour

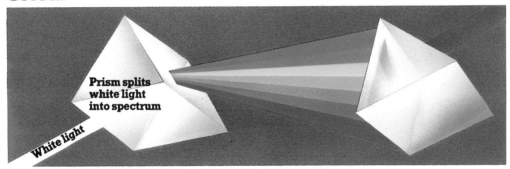

Prism splits white light into spectrum

White light

Ordinary "white" light is actually a mixture of different colours muddled together. You can use a prism to split up white light to see these colours. They fall into bands of red, orange, yellow, green, blue, indigo and violet, called a spectrum. Each colour is light of a particular wavelength; violet has a short wavelength, red a long one and the others are in between.

One colour and direction

Ordinary red light is a mix of red colours

Red laser beam is just one red colour

A red light bulb produces light of one colour but it is really a mixture of all the different wavelengths that make various reds, and probably some orange, yellow and other colours too. Laser beams are made up of light waves of identical wavelength, so they are truly just one colour or "monochromatic".

The light waves in a beam of ordinary light spread out in all directions, so the beam quickly fades as it travels. In a laser beam the light waves all travel in the same direction, forming a straight, nearly parallel "rod" of concentrated light which keeps its intensity, even over long distances.

Light waves in step

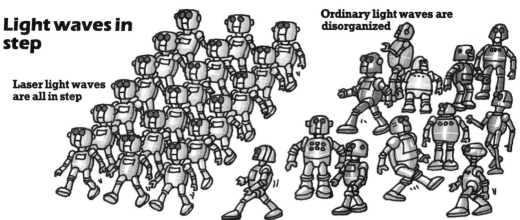

Laser light waves are all in step

Ordinary light waves are disorganized

Not only are the light waves in a laser beam all identical in wavelength and frequency, they are all in step with each other – rather like people marching. This is called being in phase. Light which is in phase is known as "coherent" light – lasers are the only source of coherent light. In ordinary light the waves are all different and so are out of phase – like a crowd wandering around a fair. This is known as "incoherent" light.

Photons

Blue, short-wavelength, high energy photons

Yellow, medium length and medium energy photons

Red, long wave, low energy photons

Light waves consist of packets of energy called photons. Each photon belonging to a particular wavelength has the same energy. But, photons of different wavelengths (colours) have different energies – the longer the wavelength, the lower the energy. So red is lower energy light than violet, with the others in between.

Laser speckle

A curious thing about laser light is that it looks sparkling and speckled with out-of-focus, tiny bright and dark spots. This is caused by the light waves in the beam bouncing off a surface. Even the most flat looking surface is a mountainous landscape when seen through a microscope. These hills and valleys put some of the coherent light waves out of step with each other. When the peaks of one wave meet with the troughs of another wave, they cancel each other out, making what you see as a tiny spot of dark. When the peaks of both meet, they add together to form what you see as a bright sparkle.

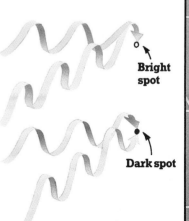

Bright spot

Dark spot

How lasers work

The name "laser" actually describes how a laser beam is made. The word is made up from the first letters of the phrase "Light Amplification by Stimulated Emission of Radiation". This phrase describes what happens inside a laser, and the process is illustrated and explained below.

A laser is a device made out of a substance that will give off light when excited by a source of energy. There are many kinds of laser, as you will see over the page, but the basic process of making a laser beam is the same for all of them. It is explained here using a gas laser, the most common kind, as an example.

Inside a laser

This is a simplified pictured of a gas laser, drawn so that you can see inside. There is a glass tube filled with gas and this is stimulated by an electric current going through it.

The electric current excites the atoms (or molecules) in the gas and they then give off or "emit" photons (light energy).

Some of the emitted photons hit other excited atoms. This causes them to give off identical photons. This is the Stimulated Emission of Radiation part of "laser".

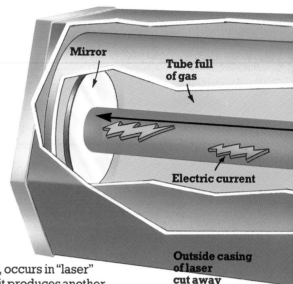

Mirror

Tube full of gas

Electric current

Outside casing of laser cut away to show inside

Amplification, which means "making bigger", occurs in "laser" because when a photon hits an excited atom, it produces another photon identical to itself, both in energy and phase. Both photons can then hit other excited atoms and produce yet more photons, which in turn make further photons, and so on.

Making a laser beam

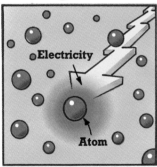

Electricity

Atom

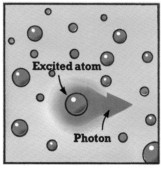

Excited atom

Photon

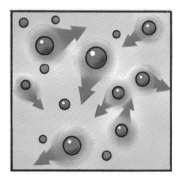

These pictures show what happens to the atoms and photons inside a laser. Electricity passes through the gas and some of its atoms absorb energy from it and become "excited".

Atoms cannot stay in this excited state and so return to normal by giving off their extra energy as a photon. This is called "spontaneous emission" and is not "lasing" – yet.

Lasing only occurs when over half the atoms are excited. This is known as an "inverted population" as it is opposite to the normal state, when few atoms are excited.

The gas tube has a mirror at each end. Some of the emitted photons hit the mirrors and are reflected back into the gas, for further amplification and stimulated emission. Only photons travelling parallel to the tube hit the mirrors. Photons travelling in other directions just go out of the tube.

The mirror at this end is only partially reflective and will let through some of the light. As long as the mirror reflects back enough photons to keep up the amplification, a beam of coherent, one colour, one direction laser light will be produced.

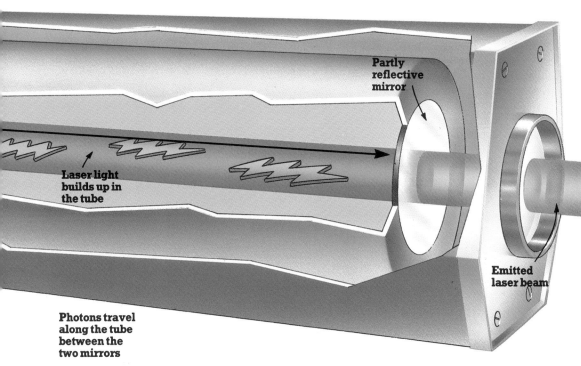

Partly reflective mirror

Laser light builds up in the tube

Emitted laser beam

Photons travel along the tube between the two mirrors

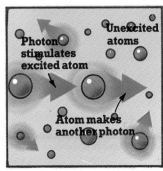

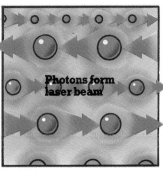

Photons form laser beam

Exciting lighting

Lasers are not the only lights to work by excitation. All light

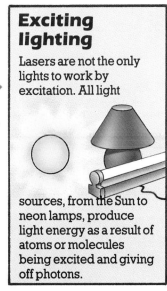

Photons hitting excited atoms produce another photon, but photons hitting unexcited atoms are lost. This is why an inverted population is necessary for lasing to occur.

The stimulated emission and amplification mean that lasing has begun. The laser light is reflected along the tube between the mirrors, producing a parallel beam, part of which is emitted.

sources, from the Sun to neon lamps, produce light energy as a result of atoms or molecules being excited and giving off photons.

7

Types of laser

The gas laser shown on the previous pages is just one type of laser. Lasers can be made from many different solids and liquids as well as from gases. The method of exciting substances to lase varies too; it can be electricity, light, chemical reaction or even another laser. This means that lasers can be matched to particular tasks. The low power laser that scans your shopping, for example, would not be at all useful for welding cars together or etching circuits on a microchip. The next four pages look at the different kinds of laser.

Gas lasers

Gas lasers are usually excited into lasing by an electric current. This picture shows a carbon dioxide (CO_2) laser with its casing off. CO_2 lasers are very common, but the sort that you are most likely to see is the helium neon (HeNe) laser. These produce a low power, red beam and are often used in schools as they are safe, small and relatively cheap. The argon (Ar) gas laser is widely used in medicine and some other gas lasers are krypton (Kr), and gold (Au) and copper (Cu) vapour where the metal has been vaporized into a kind of gas.

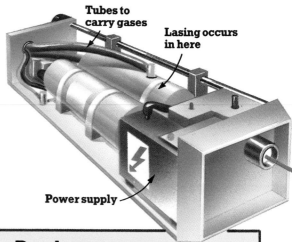

Tubes to carry gases

Lasing occurs in here

Power supply

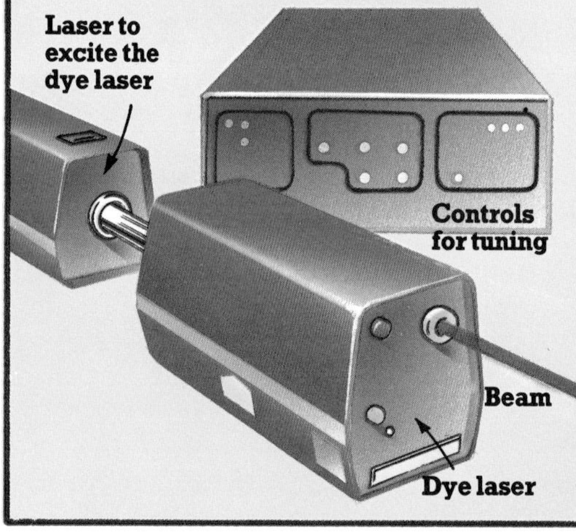

Dye lasers

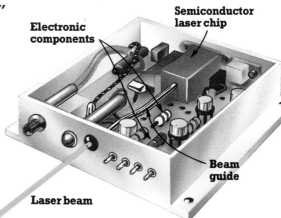

Laser to excite the dye laser

Controls for tuning

Beam

Dye laser

These are made from liquid which has been coloured by a simple dye. They produce a laser beam when excited by a very intense flash of ordinary light or another laser, as pictured here. The advantage of a dye laser is that they produce beams of different wavelengths. This happens because in a liquid the excited atoms provide a broad range of light. The laser has a prism to split this light into narrow wavelengths and so the beam can be "tuned" to different wavelengths.

Semiconductor laser "chips"

These are miniature lasers made from tiny pieces of solid material called semiconductors. (Semiconductors are used to make transistors and microchips.) Laser chips produce a tiny beam when excited by electricity. They are vital to modern telecommunications and are beginning to be used in lots of electronic equipment. This picture shows a laser chip inside a telecommunications receiver.

Semiconductor laser chip

Electronic components

Beam guide

Laser beam

Solid state lasers

Flash tube makes brilliant light

Rod of synthetic ruby crystal

"Solid state" lasers are made from rods of solid, transparent material, such as synthetic ruby and emerald. They are excited into lasing by a brilliant flash of light, pictured above. These lasers have to be made from clear crystals that will let in the light. The very first laser was a solid state ruby laser. Other solid state lasers are neodymium-yag (Nd-YAG) and neodymium in glass (Nd-glass) and they are used in industry for cutting, drilling and engraving.

Chemical lasers

When some chemicals are mixed together they react violently, producing a great deal of heat. This can excite the atoms of the chemicals into lasing. Hydrogen and fluorine react like this, producing hydrogen fluoride (HF) gas in an excited state; and a laser beam. Carbon monoxide (CO), hydrogen bromide (HBr) and hydrogen cyanide (HCN) lasers all work in this way too.

Laser beam

Laser names

Lasers are usually given the name of the substances from which they are made; carbon dioxide, argon, ruby and so on. This name is often shortened to the letters which are the symbol for the chemical, like HeNe for helium neon. The type of laser is often also mentioned, as in gold vapour laser.

Laser colours

Lasers produce beams of different colours depending upon the substance they are made from. Ruby laser beams are red, like the crystals. Every chemical produces a particular wavelength and colour. For example, sodium street lamps shine orange, neon signs are red and argon lights are greeny-blue. You can test this by carefully burning various chemicals in a flame. Salt contains sodium and will make it flare orange, potassium flares purple and copper will make it green.

Laser beams

These two pages look at the beams of different kinds of laser and how they vary. The wavelength and colour, intensity, power and length of beams all depend upon the type of laser. A laser's uses depend upon what its beam can do.

Pulsed lasers

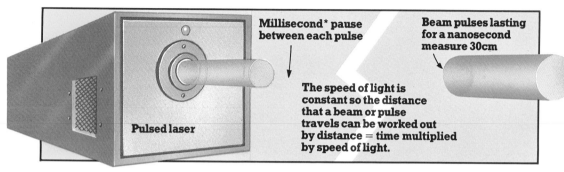

Millisecond* pause between each pulse

Beam pulses lasting for a nanosecond measure 30cm

The speed of light is constant so the distance that a beam or pulse travels can be worked out by distance = time multiplied by speed of light.

Pulsed laser

Pulsed lasers produce a beam as a series of extremely short pulses of light, rather than as a single steady beam. Lasers which are not pulsed are called continuous wave (CW) lasers. Some kinds, such as the CO_2 laser, can be either continuous or pulsed. Pulsed lasers work by emitting light only when the lasing material is at peak excitement. Some lasers produce hundreds or thousands of pulses every second and these look continuous. Others produce only one pulse every ten minutes or longer. The pulse length can vary from a few thousandths to less than a billionth of a second. The power of the light energy in a pulse is variable too.

Laser power

A laser's power is measured in watts, like light bulbs. A 10 watt bulb would hardly give enough light to read this book, but a 10 watt laser beam could be powerful enough to burn a hole right through the book. This is because laser light is concentrated in an intense beam, rather than spread out in all directions. Lasers vary in power from a few watts to many millions and are measured like this: kilowatt = thousand watts
megawatt = million watts
gigawatt = thousand million watts
terrawatt = million million watts

Pulsed lasers are the most powerful as their light energy is concentrated in rapid pulses. A low wattage continuous wave laser may be able to produce the same amount of energy as a large pulsed laser, but it will take much longer to do it.

High power, pulsed and CW lasers are used for things like drilling and cutting metals while low power CW lasers are used for playing laser discs. Medium power lasers are used for things like surgery.

* *Tiny measurements of time have these special names: millisecond = a thousandth of a sec,*

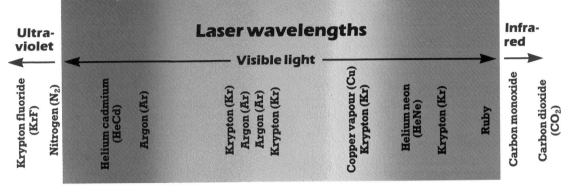

Laser wavelengths

This chart shows which lasers produce which wavelengths. Some produce beams of more than one wavelength and dye lasers can be tuned from ultra-violet to infra-red. Each wavelength is a particular, constant measurement. Visible light is between 400 and 750 nanometres (thousand-millionths of a metre) and covers the spectrum from violet to dark red. The infra-red and ultra-violet bands are much bigger than the visible band and so do not fit onto this page.

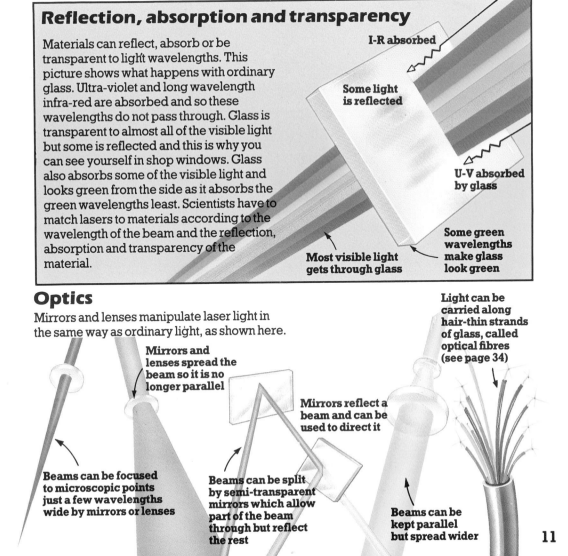

Reflection, absorption and transparency

Materials can reflect, absorb or be transparent to light wavelengths. This picture shows what happens with ordinary glass. Ultra-violet and long wavelength infra-red are absorbed and so these wavelengths do not pass through. Glass is transparent to almost all of the visible light but some is reflected and this is why you can see yourself in shop windows. Glass also absorbs some of the visible light and looks green from the side as it absorbs the green wavelengths least. Scientists have to match lasers to materials according to the wavelength of the beam and the reflection, absorption and transparency of the material.

I-R absorbed

Some light is reflected

U-V absorbed by glass

Some green wavelengths make glass look green

Most visible light gets through glass

Optics

Mirrors and lenses manipulate laser light in the same way as ordinary light, as shown here.

Light can be carried along hair-thin strands of glass, called optical fibres (see page 34)

Mirrors and lenses spread the beam so it is no longer parallel

Mirrors reflect a beam and can be used to direct it

Beams can be focused to microscopic points just a few wavelengths wide by mirrors or lenses

Beams can be split by semi-transparent mirrors which allow part of the beam through but reflect the rest

Beams can be kept parallel but spread wider

11

microsecond = a millionth, nanosecond = a thousand millionth, picosecond = a million millionth.

Lasers in industry

Lasers are used in industry to cut, drill, weld and engrave lots of things from the hardest steel and even harder diamonds to fabrics, paper and plastics. Many industrial lasers are vast, powerful machines, usually working automatically and often under computer control. The next six pages explain how lasers do these things and why they are beginning to be used instead of conventional tools like drills and saws. Perhaps lasers will one day be common DIY tools at home too.

Laser

Beam

Lens

Optical rail

Lens slides along optical rail to be focused

Working with lasers

This picture shows a helium-cadmium laser being tried out on a test bench. This small gas laser is used for laser printing (see page 33) and is about the size of a slide projector. Some industrial lasers are huge and fill a whole room.

The beam

Light comes out of the laser as a parallel beam, which is usually unable to burn a hole. It has to be focused to concentrate its power to do this.

Focusing

The beam is focused to a point with one or more lenses between the laser and the material on which it is working. The spot size and intensity of the beam is varied by adjusting the position and type of lenses. The power of the spot depends upon the kind of laser being used.

Beam focused to tiny point to drill a hole

Stability

In some applications it is important to keep the laser and optical equipment quite still, as vibrations affect the laser's accuracy. This test bench has special legs which absorb vibrations to stop them reaching the table top.

Control

Industrial lasers are often electronically controlled to produce beams of the right kind, at the right time. This is especially important with pulsed lasers. The focusing lenses and mirrors are also controlled. This makes lasers especially suitable tools for jobs which can be done automatically.

Drilling with light

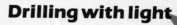

Focused sunlight

Paper

Move lens up and down

Take great care – the spot will be very hot and can burn you or cause a fire

You can test for yourself the principle of focusing light to make a hole. Use a magnifying glass to focus sunlight onto a piece of paper. Move the lens up and down to get a tiny, concentrated spot.

Choosing lasers

Lasers have to be carefully matched in power and wavelength to the job and materials they have to work on. This picture shows a laser being used to strip paint from an aircraft which needs repainting. The laser is at a wavelength that only the paint layers absorb, and so the beam burns them off. The metal beneath simply reflects the beam and is left unharmed. A laser can do this job more quickly and cheaply than other methods, such as chemical stripping.

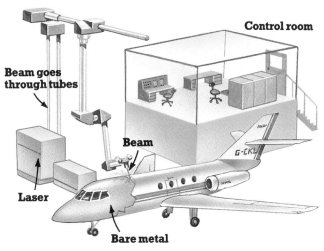

Beam goes through tubes

Control room

Beam

Laser

Bare metal

G-CKL

Directing the beam

A great advantage of the laser is that the beams can so easily be directed to where they are wanted. The laser itself is stationary but the beam can travel either along optical fibres, or simply be reflected by mirrors along a path. Light can be directed to and used in small or awkward places which would be inaccessible to ordinary tools.

The picture below shows a high power hand operated laser welding machine. The beam is directed by mirrors, inside a flexible tube. The operator can vary the power as well as freely move the beam.

Mirror

Outer casing cut away to show inside

Oxygen pipe

Lens focuses beam to a hot point

Oxygen makes beam burn hotter

Nozzle

The picture above shows the inside of a laser drilling tool that uses mirrors to guide the beam. The beam is simply reflected by the mirrors to the lens which focuses it, and then goes out through a nozzle. A jet of oxygen is used as it makes the beam hotter and more efficient for some drilling uses.

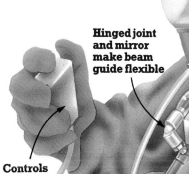

Helmet and visor

Hinged joint and mirror make beam guide flexible

Controls

Protective clothes prevent sparks burning the operator

Beam guide

Drilling and cutting

The most common industrial uses for lasers are cutting and drilling. An advantage of a laser beam is that as it is simply powerful light, it cannot wear out or clog up, as saws and drill bits do. Lasers are very fast and clean and also more accurate and precise than conventional tools.

How lasers make holes

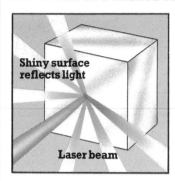

Shiny surface reflects light

Laser beam

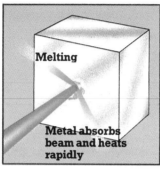

Melting

Metal absorbs beam and heats rapidly

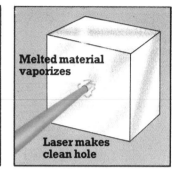

Melted material vaporizes

Laser makes clean hole

The focused beam heats the surface of the material. Shiny things like metals reflect much of the beam at first, so heat slowest.

The surface starts to melt. Metals begin to heat rapidly now as the surface is dulled by melting and there is less reflection.

Almost immediately, the melted material gets so hot it boils away – vaporizes. The beam goes in deeper, making a clean hole.

Drilling

A laser drills by vaporizing the material in a hole as fast as possible. This is best done by pulsed lasers as they deliver short, high energy beams. The material in a hole is completely removed by the vaporization. With an ordinary mechanical drill bit, tiny pieces of waste material are forced out of the hole. This "swarf" clogs up machinery and cuts workers' hands. A laser leaves a clean hole with no swarf.

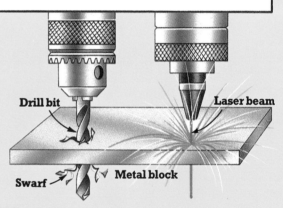

Drill bit

Laser beam

Swarf

Metal block

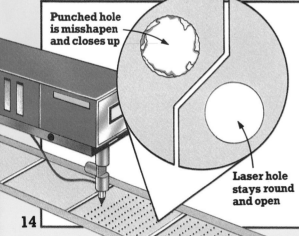

Punched hole is misshapen and closes up

Laser hole stays round and open

Laser holes

The picture on the left shows a laser drilling tiny holes in stretchy plastic bandages and compares a laser hole with a punched hole. Lasers are especially good at cutting and drilling this sort of material and fibrous things like paper and cloth, as they are "non contact" tools. This means that the beam does not actually touch the surface it is working, so does not push it out of shape. Punched holes and cuts tend to close up, as the materials are squashed or stretched in the process.

Cutting

Lasers use the same principle for cutting as for drilling, but either the laser, or the material, moves so the beam traces a path and makes a cut. This cut is called the "kerf" and it is very clean and narrow as the laser cuts by vaporization. The area on either side of the kerf is often slightly damaged by the beam. This is known as the "HAZ", short for Heat Affected Zone. The laser is controlled to keep the HAZ as small as possible. The kerf and HAZ cut in foam rubber are illustrated in the circle below.

Robot arm

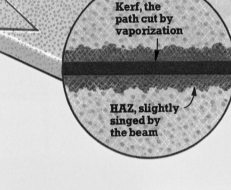

Beam guide

Kerf, the path cut by vaporization

HAZ, slightly singed by the beam

The picture above shows an industrial robot which is cutting complex shapes out of foam rubber, using a laser. The laser is behind the robot as it is too big to fix onto it. The beam travels along the guide tube, reflected by mirrors inside. Both the laser and robot are computer controlled, working to a program that tells the robot what shape to trace and turns the laser on and off.

Shape cutter

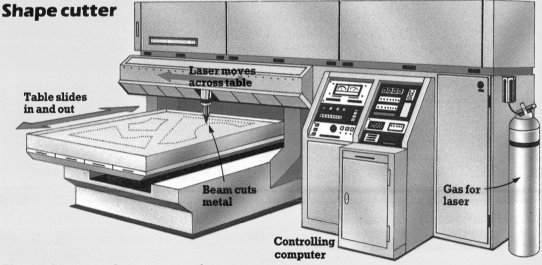

Laser moves across table

Table slides in and out

Beam cuts metal

Gas for laser

Controlling computer

This machine uses a laser to cut out shapes in metal sheeting. The metal is fixed to a motor driven table which slides in and out under the laser. The beam is directed by mirrors through a nozzle and is driven in the opposite direction across the table. The shapes to be cut out are programmed into the computer which controls the movements of both the laser and table.

Engraving and welding

The precision, accuracy and easy control of laser beams make them excellent tools for engraving, welding and treating the surfaces of various materials, as well as for cutting and drilling. These two pages show how lasers are used for these tasks.

Computer controlled engraving

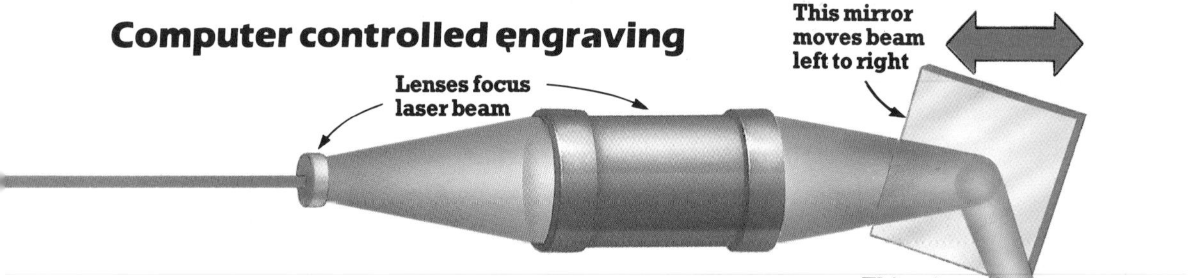

This mirror moves beam left to right

Lenses focus laser beam

Engraving is similar to cutting, except the beam does not go all the way through. This picture shows how a computer-controlled laser engraver works. The beam is engraving letters and numbers onto an electronic component.

This mirror moves beam up and down

The characters to be engraved are typed on a computer keyboard, together with instructions about size, shape and style of printing. Instructions about the speed, depth and power of beam are also given.

Controlling computer

Laser beam

The beam is focused by lenses and made to follow a path by moving mirrors. These direct and focus the laser beam on the surface of the component, making it engrave the correct characters. The beam itself moves to trace the path. This sort of set up can also be used to engrave pictures and all kinds of shapes as well as letters and numbers.

Electronic component

MN110.24
N-3

Welding

This picture shows a laser beam welding two sheets of steel together. The beam melts – but does not vaporize – a cone-shaped area of metal as it moves across the join between the two sheets. The molten metal from the two sheets mixes together and quickly solidifies when the beam moves away, to form a strong weld.

Laser welding is very fast. Big, powerful CO_2 lasers can weld steel of 2.5cm thickness at a rate of two metres a second. It is also very accurate and clean as the HAZ is small.

Laser beam

Molten metals mix and solidify as laser moves on

Cone-shaped molten area goes down through steel

Metal away from beam is unaffected by beam, so does not scorch or melt

Spot welding

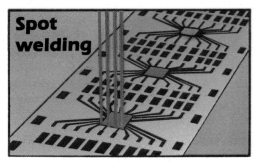

This laser beam has been split into four and is welding microchips into their cases. Lasers are good for this, being precise and accurate even at such tiny sizes. Another advantage is that the beam cannot contaminate the chip as it does not touch it.

Pulse welding

Each ridge is formed by a beam pulse

This metal case contains explosives. The end is sealed onto the sides by a pulsed laser which makes a ridged seam. The heat and depth of the beam are so precisely controlled that the explosive, only a millimetre below the weld, is unaffected.

Vacuum welding

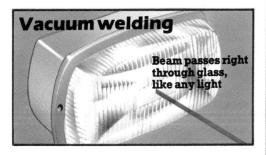

Beam passes right through glass, like any light

As it is a form of light, a laser beam can do things that are impossible with conventional tools. This beam is welding the filament inside a car headlamp. The beam goes through the glass and is unaffected by the vacuum or special gas inside.

Surface treatments

Lots of materials can be improved if they are heated and very often this treatment is needed only on the surface. Steel, for example, can be made harder for longer life by rapid heating followed by rapid cooling. This process changes the actual composition of a very thin layer of the metal at the surface. The picture below shows a knife edge being hardened in this way, by laser. The same treatment is also used on engine parts for cars and planes to stop them wearing out quickly.

Rapid heating where beam hits steel

Rapid cooling as beam moves on

Another treatment is heating, followed by slow cooling – this is known as "annealing". It is a process used on the special crystals of semiconductors used to make microchips. These crystals have to be pure and free from imperfections. Unfortunately they often have natural strains and cracks in the material that forms the crystal. By heating the surface and allowing it to cool slowly, these crystal defects can be broken and allowed to re-form.

This picture shows the changes that annealing can cause in the crystal structure and how it smooths out the surface of the semiconductor.

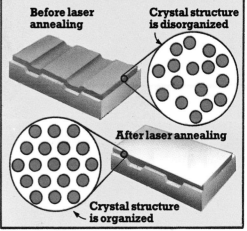

Before laser annealing

Crystal structure is disorganized

After laser annealing

Crystal structure is organized

Laser discs

One of the places that you may come across lasers in the future is when playing music and video discs. A new kind of disc, which is recorded and played by laser beam, has been developed. They have silvery, mirror-like surfaces which reflect light in a rainbow spectrum, like the one pictured here. Video discs are about the size of an LP and hold both pictures and sound. Audio discs are sound only, much smaller and often known as compact or digital discs. These two pages look at how laser discs work and what is special about them.

How laser discs work

Laser disc

This picture shows a laser disc being scanned by a semiconductor laser chip. Some players use small HeNe lasers instead. It also shows the optical equipment of lenses, mirrors and so on which are inside the player.

The laser disc has a very reflective metallic surface, covered by a protective coating of clear plastic. There are microscopically tiny indentations in this surface, called "pits" and the plain areas in between are "flats". The circle on the right shows the pits and flats greatly magnified.

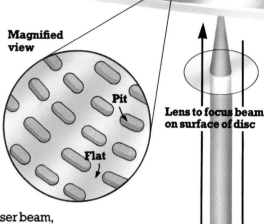

Magnified view

Pit

Flat

Lens to focus beam on surface of disc

The player spins the disc and scans it with the laser beam, which moves straight across the disc from the centre to the edge. The shiny surface reflects the beam back into the player, where it is picked up by an electronic device. This produces an electrical signal when it detects light.

Mirror bends beam

The pits and flats on the disc reflect the laser beam differently, producing a varying beam. This in turn makes the detector produce a varying electrical signal, which the player de-codes back into video pictures and sounds.

Beam to disc

Beam reflected by disc

Detector

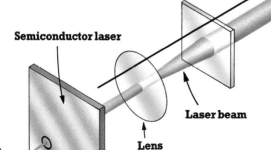

Semiconductor laser

This lens bends only the beam reflected by the disc

Lens

Laser beam

Lens

Reflected beam has been varied by pits and flats

Recording laser discs

The pits and flats are originally made by a laser beam, controlled by the electrical signals recorded with video cameras and microphones. Only one disc is recorded in this way and it acts as a "master" to make moulds from which all the copies are pressed. You can't use laser discs for recording at home.

Video discs

Video disc player

This picture shows a video disc player and discs, with an ordinary TV to show the pictures. Each side of the disc holds up to an hour of video, or 54,000 still pictures.

Why laser discs are special

The way that laser discs are played and recorded makes them different from other kinds of records. Their plastic coating makes them amazingly tough and they can be thrown about – even stamped on – without much ill effect and will play even if scratched and dirty. This is because the laser beam is precisely focused only on the reflective surface, as pictured below. Any imperfections on the clear, outer layer are out of focus and ignored.

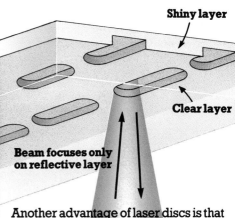

Another advantage of laser discs is that they never wear out. There is no physical contact between the disc and player – only a beam of light, too weak to harm either. Even the players are more reliable as there are fewer mechanical parts to break down.

Digital discs

Audio discs are also known as compact discs because of their small size and as digital discs because they are recorded using computer processing. Digital recordings are better quality than the ordinary kind as they can deal with a wider range of sounds. Many problems such as background hissing and crackling are actually created by conventional recording techniques and so avoided on digital discs. Video discs are not digital.

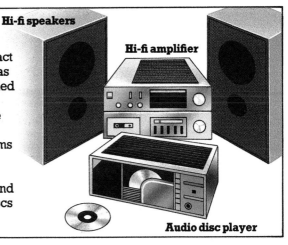

Medical lasers

Lasers can drill, cut and weld not only metals and plastics, but also people. They are being used in many kinds of medical operations and proving to be very efficient. Lasers are replacing the surgeon's scalpel and this is often called "bloodless surgery" as the heat of the beam seals up blood vessels around the cut and prevents bleeding. Beams are also used in operations to destroy growths. There is little or no pain and healing is faster than in conventional surgery.

These two pages show some of the laser's many medical uses.

Inside the stomach

This picture shows a laser beam operating on an ulcer inside a patient's stomach. The beam travels through an optical fibre which is part of an instrument called an endoscope.

The endoscope

Endoscopes are made from bundles of optical fibres and thin tubes, put together into a cable about as thick as a finger. They are slim enough to pass down the patient's throat, without causing too much discomfort. The extra tubes provide air, water and suction to clean the area on which the beam is working.

The laser

This operation is being done by an argon laser which produces a green beam. Nd-YAG lasers are also used for surgery but as they produce an invisible, infra-red beam, they have to be mixed with a red helium neon laser beam, so that the surgeon can see where it is.

Ulcers

Ulcers are arteries that bleed into the stomach. The laser treats them by heating the end of the artery and welding the opening shut. The weld is made by a tiny scar which forms over the burn. The tissue surrounding the ulcer is not affected by the laser, as the beam is precisely focused on the artery.

Lasers can also be used to remove unwanted growths such as tumours, stones and cysts which form on internal organs.

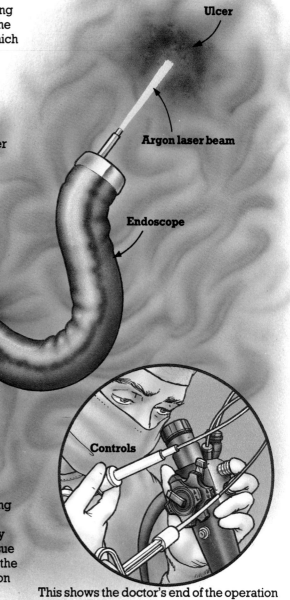

Ulcer

Argon laser beam

Endoscope

Controls

This shows the doctor's end of the operation and the controls for the endoscope and laser. The doctor can see inside the stomach via optical fibres in the endoscope.

Skin treatment

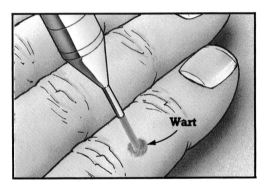

The precision of a laser is also used on the outside of the body. They remove warts, and other growths, leaving the skin around untouched. Lasers are so accurate they can peel skin away in very thin layers

Tooth decay

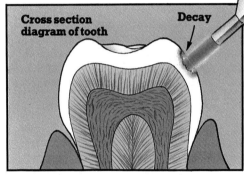

Dentists are beginning to test lasers for drilling decay from teeth. Only the dark, rotten areas absorb the laser beam. The white, healthy parts of the tooth reflect it and are left unaffected, as shown above.

Eye surgery

The laser's most common medical use is in eye surgery. Some eye defects occur when the retina is detached from the back of the eye. A laser can weld the retina back into place without the need to cut open the eye. The beam passes straight through the eye ball without affecting it, just as ordinary light does. The beam is focused on the retina by the lens of the eye itself. A small heat scar results and makes the weld.

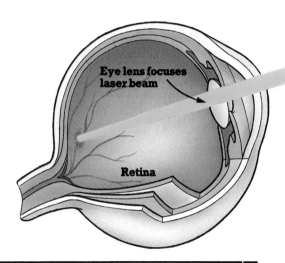

Removing marks

Lasers can remove markings such as tattoos and some birth marks. The large red birth marks known as "port wine stains" are the most easily treated. A green wavelength argon laser is used as the red coloured areas of the birth mark will absorb more of the beam than the normal coloured skin. This picture shows a red beam being used on a green tattoo. The laser burns away tiny areas of the marking so that new, uncoloured skin will grow to replace it. The treatment is almost painless but takes a long time as only small areas can be treated in one session.

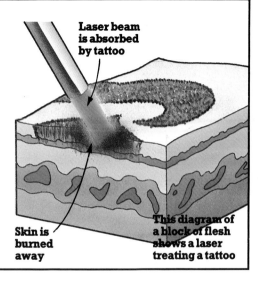

Holograms

A hologram is a kind of photograph, made with a laser and recorded on a flat plate of photographic film or glass. The unique thing about holograms is that they have a three-dimensional (3D) image which looks solid. The image seems to hang in space; either in front of the plate or behind it or even right across it. As you move in relation to the hologram you get a different view of the image, just as you do when looking at a real object. Holograms are so convincing, you feel as if you could grab the image or put your hand right into the picture. The next six pages look at what holograms are, how they are made and their uses.

Designed by Dicken Eames

Produced by Light Fantastic (UK) Ltd.

This is a photograph of a hologram. It is very difficult to show the 3D nature of holograms in a book, which is 2D.

The third dimension

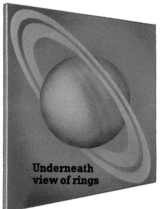

Underneath view of rings

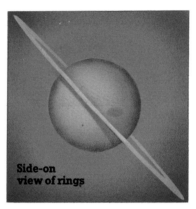

Side-on view of rings

Top view of rings

These pictures illustrate three views of a hologram of a model of Saturn. The view of the planet and its rings changes as you move in relation to the hologram. You can see the rings from underneath, side-on and above. The whole image changes as you move, unlike a photograph which looks the same no matter where you are. This realistic changing image is called "parallax".

How holograms work

You only see things because light is reflected from them and detected by your eyes. A hologram looks so realistic because it is an exact recording of the light waves reflected from an object. When the image is reconstructed it reflects light in just the same way as the object originally did. This gives the hologram its convincing illusion of reality. Light reaching your eyes from the hologram is the same as that from the real object.

Real object   **Hologram**

All-round view

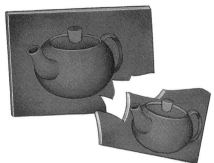

Whole camera can be seen from different angles

Cylindrical plate

A flat plate has only limited parallax, rather as a window does. By recording holograms from all angles on a cylindrical plate, it is possible to make a 360° holographic image. The image seems to float in the cylinder.

Whole image

The word hologram means "whole picture". If a plate is broken, each piece has the whole image on it, not just the part it showed originally. The view, though, is more restricted.

Looking at holograms

Unreconstructed hologram

Reflection hologram

Transmission hologram

A hologram looks like a fuzzy blur until lit by a light. This is called "reconstruction" and makes the image visible. Some can only be seen when lit by a laser but most need only a spotlight, although it may have to be at a particular angle. There are two kinds of hologram and they differ in the way they are reconstructed. Reflection holograms are lit by light shining on the front of the plate. Transmission holograms by light shining through the plate. In both cases it is the light from the plate that makes you see the image.

Holographic colour

Holograms do not give true colour reproduction. Their colour depends upon the colour of the laser used to make the hologram. Multi-coloured images are created by using different lasers to light different parts of the objects being pictured.

A different kind of multi-coloured hologram, called a rainbow hologram, changes colour as you move in relation to it. It covers the whole spectrum from red to violet.

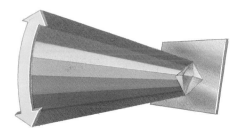

This picture shows how a rainbow hologram changes colour. Holographic colours are very brilliant and vivid because they are made from pure, one wavelength light. **23**

Making holograms

Holography is a photographic process in which lenses and mirrors are used to direct and focus a laser beam. The image of an object is recorded on a plate, which is covered by an emulsion of light sensitive chemicals. The plate is exposed both from direct laser light and laser light reflected by the object. Chemical changes take place in the emulsion when the two beams meet, making a permanent record of the object. Ordinary film records a photograph by chemical changes too. The picture below shows how the equipment is set up to make a hologram of a telephone.

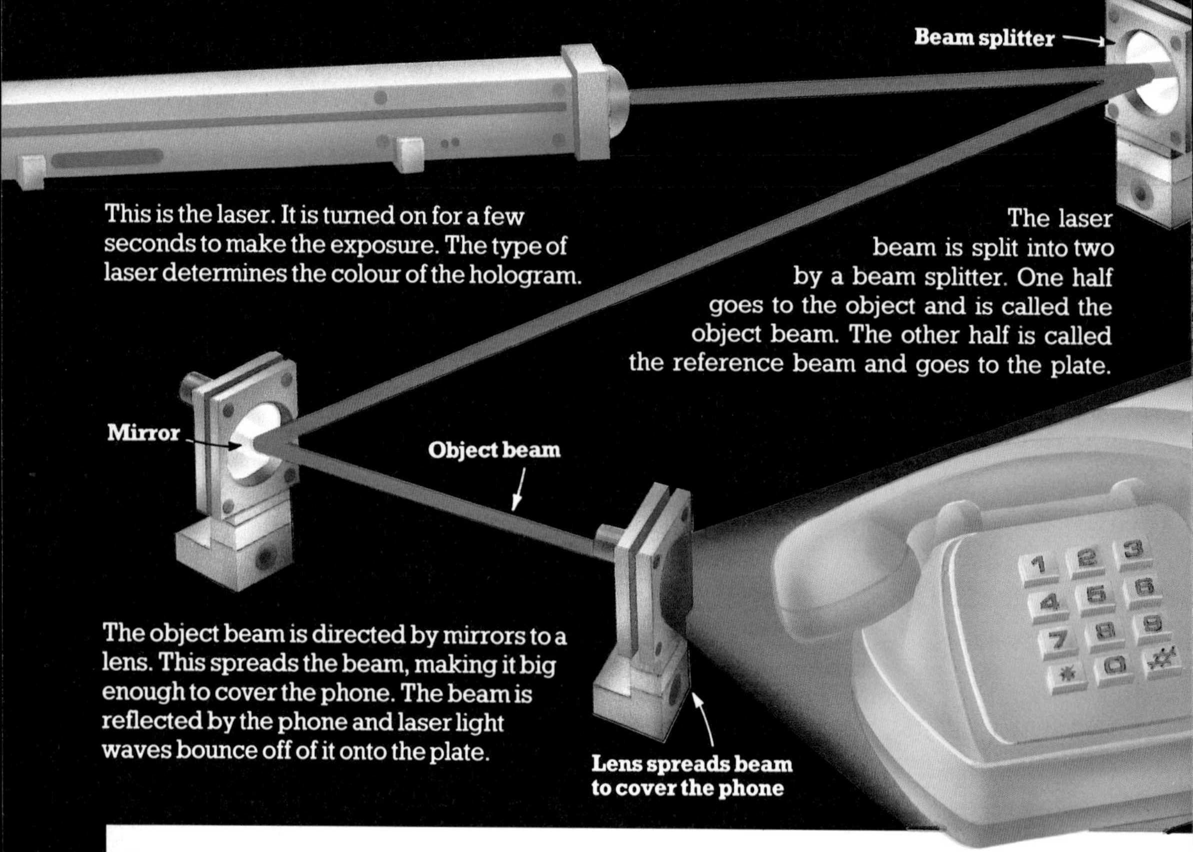

Beam splitter ⟶

This is the laser. It is turned on for a few seconds to make the exposure. The type of laser determines the colour of the hologram.

The laser beam is split into two by a beam splitter. One half goes to the object and is called the object beam. The other half is called the reference beam and goes to the plate.

Mirror

Object beam

The object beam is directed by mirrors to a lens. This spreads the beam, making it big enough to cover the phone. The beam is reflected by the phone and laser light waves bounce off of it onto the plate.

Lens spreads beam to cover the phone

Interference patterns

The interference pattern made on the plate by the laser beams is a record of the object. The lightwaves in the reflected object beam are out of phase with those of the undisturbed reference beam. The differences between them are "measurements" of the object, in lightwaves.

You can make a kind of interference pattern by dropping two stones into water. The two sets of ripples disturb each other and make an interference pattern where they meet.

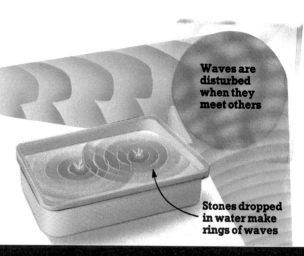

Waves are disturbed when they meet others

Stones dropped in water make rings of waves

Holography table

It is vital to keep everything as still as possible – any vibrations, even sound waves, will blur the finished hologram. The set-up is usually put on a special table made out of sand and inflated tyre tubes, resting on a concrete floor, to absorb unwanted vibrations.

– **Mirror**

Reference beam

The reference beam is also directed by mirrors to a spreading lens. It is focused through the lens onto the plate.

Lens spreads beam to cover the plate

Plate covered with photographic emulsion

Light reflected from phone has information of its shape

The reference beam can be directed to either side of the plate – the same side as the object beam, or the opposite side, as shown here. It depends whether a reflection or transmission hologram is being made (see next page).

The reference beam and the reflected object beam meet at the plate. The reference beam is still in its original form. But, the object beam is a reflection of the phone, so the light waves of the two beams are no longer in phase (see page 5). As lasers are the only source of coherent (in phase) light it is impossible to make holograms without them. The two beams mix and make an "interference pattern" (see below) in the light sensitive chemicals on the plate. This is what is reconstructed to make the image when the plate is lit up.

Constructive interference

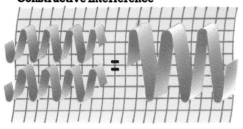

Destructive interference

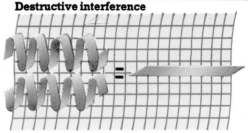

The two pictures above show what happens when two sets of lightwaves meet. If the peaks of one coincide with the peaks of the other, they add together to make a wave double the original size. This is called "constructive interference". If peaks coincide with

troughs they cancel each other out. This is called "destructive interference". In-between stages make waves of varying sizes. It is these combined waves that make the fuzzy ripples of the interference pattern, visible on the plate.

Making holograms . . . 2

After being exposed, the holographic plate has to be processed in a similar way to photographic film. The image must then be reconstructed by a beam shining from the same direction as the reference beam that made the hologram. The two pictures below show the differences in the making of transmission and reflection holograms.

Reflection hologram

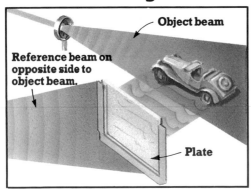

If the reference beam is shone onto the opposite side of the plate to the object the hologram will be a reflection hologram, visible by light reflecting off it.

Transmission hologram

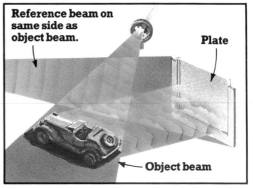

If the reference beam was on the same side as the object then the plate will have to be lit from that side and will be a transmission hologram.

Holographic movies

At the moment holography is not practical for making proper moving pictures. It is possible to make a simple hologram "movie" by using a sequence of holograms side by side along a plate. You see the image "move" as you walk past. This sort of hologram is usually made by shining lasers through recorded cine film, as it is necessary to have hundreds of images to show even a tiny movement, like a kick or wave of the hand.

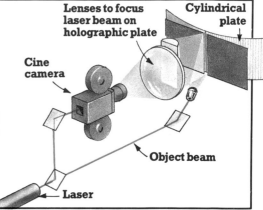

Multiple images

Several images can be recorded on top of each other on a single plate by changing the angle of the reference beam used for each. The different pictures will become visible when the angle of the viewing beam is changed – as happens when the viewer moves in relation to the plate. This is one way of making a simple animated hologram, which works rather like a flick picture.

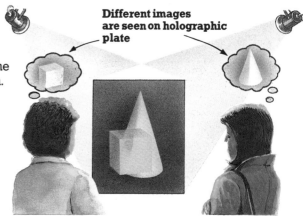

Three ways of 3D

Real image hologram

Image plane hologram

Virtual image hologram

A holographic plate is a flat sheet but the image can appear in different places in relation to it. A hologram can seem to sink backwards – this is known as a "virtual image". More dramatically, the image can project into space in front of the plate, springing out at you – this is called a "real image". The image may also straddle across the plate, half of it sinking back, half of it coming forwards – known as an "image plane". The pictures above show these three kinds of hologram.

Making a real image hologram

The holographic set up shown on the previous pages will produce virtual image holograms. Real image and image plane holograms are not made directly from a real object, but from a virtual image hologram.

To do this, the image is reconstructed but lit from the wrong side; so a transmission hologram is lit from in front, a reflection hologram from behind. The image appears hanging in front of the plate – as a real image – but it is inside out and back to front. This is known as a "pseudoscopic"* image. These pictures show how a hologram of the letter F changes when pseudoscopic. The hologram made from the pseudoscopic image will also be a virtual image, but when it is lit from the wrong side, it will be a real image hologram and the right way round. This is because when something that is already inside out is turned inside out, it becomes right way round again.

27

* Pronounced syou-do-scopick

Using holograms

Holography is now at about the stage that photography reached around 1900. Perhaps in the next century you will be taking holographic snaps, reading holographic magazines and watching 3D laser TV. You can already see holograms in galleries, museums, exhibitions, buy them to hang on your wall or made into jewellery and even find them printed in books and magazines. One limitation to holography is the fact that holograms are always exactly the same size as the original object. So, holograms of things bigger than the largest plates, about a metre square, cannot be made and reductions are not possible either. These pages show some uses for holograms.

Holograms can make very impressive advertising displays. This real image of a hand and diamond bracelet was used by a jeweller's shop in New York. The image seemed to hang a metre out from the window.

Holograms can be printed, by a special process, onto silvery plastic. They are used for books, LP covers, and even sweet wrappers. Printed holograms are not so clear or detailed as those on plates.

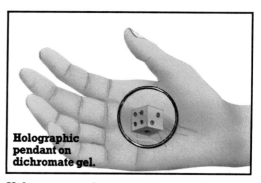

Holographic pendant on dichromate gel.

Holograms can be recorded on a light-sensitive jelly called dichromate gel. The hologram is covered by glass to make jewellery, or used on other clear containers such as jars.

Telephone call by hologram

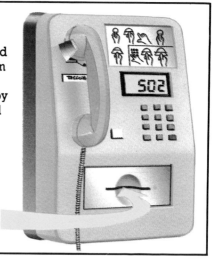

This credit card can be used with new, computerized pay phones. The card has a strip of printed hologram on the back. The hologram is not a picture, but a special forgery proof pattern. The strip is scanned by an infra-red optical device in the phone. While a call is being made the scanner slowly destroys the strip as the credit is used up. The phone controls the scanner's speed, according to the cost of the call and shows how much credit is left on the card at the end.

Nuclear safety

This picture shows a hologram of the core of a nuclear reactor used to generate electricity. Scientists have to carry out safety checks, looking for cracks and other faults. They cannot do this by getting close to the core as it is dangerously radioactive. A hologram provides all the information that the real thing could and is so accurate that the image can even be examined under a microscope.

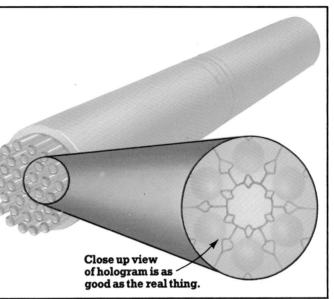

Close up view of hologram is as good as the real thing.

Stress check

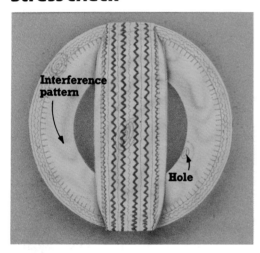

Interference pattern

Hole

This picture is a hologram of a motor car tyre. The swirling patterns show the stresses that build up in the tyre when it moves. They are recorded by making two holograms on one plate using a pulsed laser. One is made when the tyre is still, the other when it is moving. The two images do not exactly overlap and this creates an interference pattern in the hologram. The pattern indicates areas of stress and can show faults, such as holes or weak spots. Tyres are not the only things to be tested with this technique. All kinds of things, from beer cans to jet turbines, have to be measured for stress and can be checked in this way.

Credit card security

T 1350   DC

Embossed holograms are being used to make credit cards forgery proof. As holograms are difficult to make, forgers cannot copy a card which has a hologram of the company's symbol on it.

Keeping records

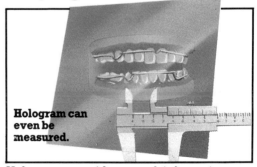

Hologram can even be measured.

Holograms provide as much information as a solid object, yet take up much less room, being thin, flat plates. They are being used as visual records for many things from dentures to art treasures.

Laser light shows

Although lasers are important to areas as diverse as engineering and medicine, they are not especially visible when being used in these ways. You are most likely actually to see lasers at pop concerts, on TV and in films, in discos, as street decorations and at shows devoted just to laser light. They are used in these ways because laser light is incredibly beautiful and can make wonderful effects. These pages picture and explain some of the laser light effects that you may see.

Solid light

Sheets and tunnels of light can be made by shining the beams onto clouds and mist bellowed out by smoke machines. The effect is created by particles in the clouds reflecting the light.

Rhythm pulsing

Lasers can be pulsed in time with the beat of pop music, as pictured above. This is done by an electronic device which uses the music's electrical signals to control the beams.

Fans

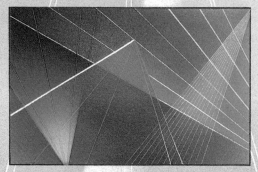

Huge fan shapes of light are made by lenses that spread and divide the beams. They can be moved up and down and rolled from side to side to make interwoven patterns of light.

Computer control

The lasers and optical equipment are controlled by computer from the console pictured here. The operator can work everything manually but most shows are so complex they are usually preprogrammed to create the effects.

The effects are done using mirrors and lenses to split, spread, move and direct the laser beams. There are huge projectors to house all this optical equipment and the lasers. The lasers used for light shows are safe when used properly, but could cause burns or damage eyes if shone directly at people.

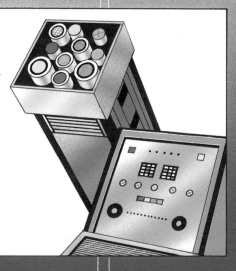

Producing patterns

These pictures show the kind of patterns laser beams can make.

The beams are directed into these complex paths by special lenses, prisms and mirrors which rotate and vibrate to direct and "shape" the laser beam.

The laser beams do not actually make these shapes. They trace round the path so fast that the eye is fooled into seeing the shapes as if they are hanging in mid-air.

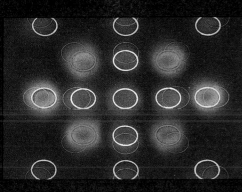

This technique can even be used to make light writing and draw pictures. Perhaps lasers will one day be used for signwriting and advertisements.

Colour mixing

Krypton lasers which produce beams of four colours – red, gold, green and blue – are often used in light shows. The colours can be separated and mixed by directing the beam through a prism which splits the light into different wavelengths. Dye lasers are also popular as they can be "tuned" to produce lots of wavelengths and so almost any colour.

Silhouettes

Light cannot pass through solid objects so putting something in the way of a beam can produce a dramatic result.

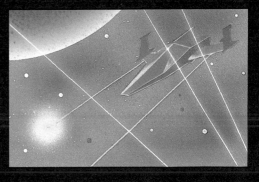

Lasers are often used in films to create the effects shown on these pages. But the death rays from "laser" guns and swords of sci-fi adventures are usually painted on the film, often by hand.

31

Laser communications

An important and fast growing use for lasers is the storing, processing and communication of information. Lasers now transmit phone calls, TV broadcasts, computer data, and messages to satellites and submarines. They also store and read information on optical discs, bar codes and credit cards, and are used in printing books, newspapers and magazines. These two pages look at how lasers can do these things.

Satellite signals

Laser beams going straight through the air are not practical communications links, as they are badly affected by clouds and fog. However, they are important for sending signals to and between satellites in space, where there is no weather. A laser beam is almost impossible to intercept and so they are very important to military users.

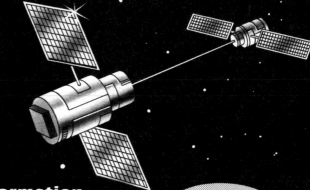

How beams carry information

In order to be stored or transmitted, all information – sounds, text, pictures or computer data – is turned into an electrical signal. This signal is an electrical form of the original, a microphone turns the varying sounds of your voice into a varying current of electricity which can travel along wires or be recorded. If a laser is stimulated by this electrical signal, it produces a beam that varies in the same way as the signal, and so in intensity in the same way as the original information. The beam can be used to carry the information, or store it on laser readable optical discs.

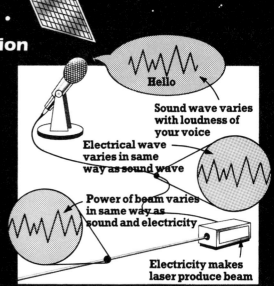

Hello

Sound wave varies with loudness of your voice

Electrical wave varies in same way as sound wave

Power of beam varies in same way as sound and electricity

Electricity makes laser produce beam

Optical fibres

Using light to carry information only became practical with the invention of optical fibres. These are flexible glass rods, as thin as hair, which act as "wires" for light. They work by totally reflecting the light inside so that none of it leaks out. Optical fibres are smaller than ordinary wires, yet light can carry much more information than radio waves and electrical signals, and so can provide more phone lines and TV channels. Optical fibre phone lines cannot be bugged or tapped.

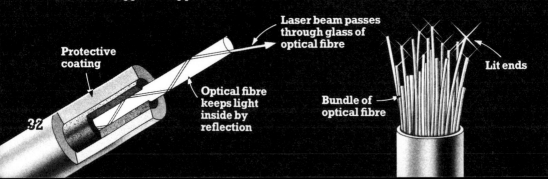

Laser beam passes through glass of optical fibre

Protective coating

Optical fibre keeps light inside by reflection

Bundle of optical fibre

Lit ends

Optical storage

The technology used for storing pictures and sounds on laser discs (see pages 18-19) can be used for other kinds of information too. Small, laser readable optical discs, like those shown here, may be widely used for storing computer data and software in the future. They are more hardwearing than the magnetic disks and tapes used now, and can hold more information.

Laser printing

Lasers are being used for printing in several ways. This book was printed using sheets of metal, known as printing plates, with the words and pictures engraved on the surface. Lasers can be used to engrave the plates (see page 16). Printed type can also be produced with a technique very similar to this laser engraving. The beam is controlled in the same way to make letters, but instead of cutting a groove it is shone onto photographic paper. The laser exposes the paper and the places where the beam traced a path will become the dark marks of type when the paper is processed.

Another printing task for lasers is scanning or "reading" pages and turning the information into an electrical signal – (see bar codes below). This signal can then be transmitted to distant offices for printing.

Paper

Laser

Beam

Bar codes

Lasers are probably at work in your local supermarket or library, reading bar codes. A bar code is computerized information, encoded in a pattern of light and dark lines. A laser reads these lines by reflecting a beam off the pattern back to a detector in the "wand". The light and dark stripes make different reflections. The information is then decoded by computer. Bar codes can be used to store data of all kinds, from music to food prices.

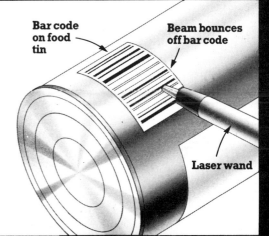

Bar code on food tin

Beam bounces off bar code

Laser wand

Measuring with lasers

Skyscraper

Lasers are being used to help make maps, build skyscrapers and measure distances both huge and minute. The properties of laser light make it very useful for these jobs, which are explained on these pages.

Laser beam is parallel and perfectly vertical

Laser plumb-line

As a laser beam is parallel and straight, even over large distances, it can be used as a kind of plumb-line or spirit-level to make sure that things are straight or level. The picture on the right shows a tall office block being aligned with a vertical laser beam during building. The beam's angle is monitored by special electronic equipment.

Laser tape measures

B

A

Distance A to B equals time multiplied by 300 million metres

A laser produces a beam of light and all light travels at a constant speed of 300 million m/s, in the air. So, a distance can be measured accurately by timing the passage of a laser beam between two places. The beam is timed with precise electronic equipment which also works out the correct distance.

Laser to the Moon

Reflector

Laser beam

Earth

The distance between the Earth and Moon has been measured by a laser beam, bounced back to Earth from a reflector left on the Moon. Although laser light is parallel over shorter distances, the beam spreads to about a kilometre wide over this vast distance.

Mapping the sea-bed

◄─── Laser beam

Green light lasers are used to measure the depth of water and map the sea-bed. Light of this wavelength can penetrate water to a depth of several hundred metres. The laser is carried by a helicopter flying just above the surface. The beam bounces back to electronic timing devices.

Aligning pipes

Beneath our cities, countryside and seas are networks of pipes which carry essential services such as oil, gas, water, sewerage and communications cables for TV and phones. Engineers use the straight beams of lasers to help accurately lay and align these pipes. This picture shows one being used in a drainage sewer.

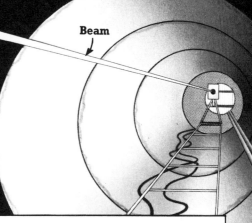

Beam

Microscopic measurements

An important property of a laser beam is that it is light of just one wavelength. Minute measurements are made by counting the number of wavelengths between one point and another. This is done with an "interferometer".

The interferometer works by splitting a laser beam in two, reflecting each part onto a different mirror and then recombining them into one beam. The two parts of the recombined beam will be out of phase, unless the difference between them is an exact whole number of wavelengths. This means that if one mirror is moved, a pattern of light and dark interference fringes is produced (see pages 24-25). A detector in the interferometer counts these fringes to work out the difference between the two beams, and therefore the distance by multiplying the number of fringes by the wavelength.

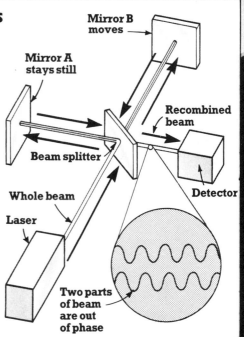

Mirror B
moves

Mirror A
stays still

Recombined
beam

Beam splitter

Whole beam

Detector

Laser

Two parts
of beam
are out
of phase

Sky heights

Laser beam →

Cloud height can be difficult to measure, especially at night, but it is very important to aircraft pilots. Some light wavelengths are reflected particularly well by the water droplets in clouds and lasers are now used at some airports in foggy or cloudy weather.

Reflective satellite

Corner-cubes

LAGEOS satellite

This satellite, called LAGEOS, reflects laser beams back to Earth. It is covered with special lenses, called corner-cubes, which send beams back to exactly where they came from. It is used to study tiny movements in the Earth's crust and the slow drift of the continents.

Laser weapons

When the laser was first invented, it appeared in science fiction as a deadly weapon. Many films still show "laser" swords, ray-guns and space cannons in action. So far, laser weapons are still mostly fiction, despite the fact that beams can be dangerous. Secret research is being carried out in several countries to make lasers that will destroy planes, missiles and satellites. The problem with this is that such lasers would have to be very powerful and extremely large – so not easy to manoeuvre or use. However, lasers are being used by the military in several ways other than as deadly rays, as shown on these pages.

Airborne laser lab

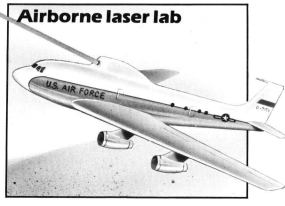

This is a picture of one of the few real laser weapons, built by the USA. It is a converted airliner housing a giant carbon dioxide laser. In tests in 1983 it shot down five missiles.

Shooting in the dark

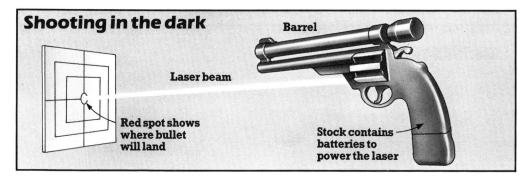

Barrel

Laser beam

Red spot shows where bullet will land

Stock contains batteries to power the laser

This ordinary looking hand gun has a helium neon laser mounted under the barrel. A slight touch on the trigger activates the laser and throws a spot of red laser light on the target. The spot is visible in the dark but it also helps with taking aim in daylight as the bullet lands exactly where the spot is. So the gun can be fired accurately "from the hip".

Range finding binoculars

These binoculars are mounted on an anti-tank gun and use a laser to measure the distance between it and a target. The soldier focuses the binoculars on the tank and sets off the laser. An invisible beam hits the target and bounces back into the binoculars where an electronic timer calculates how far away the target is (see pages 34-35 for more on this). The distance is shown in one of the eyepieces. If the tank is within range the soldier knows that by keeping it lined up through the binoculars he will make a direct hit.

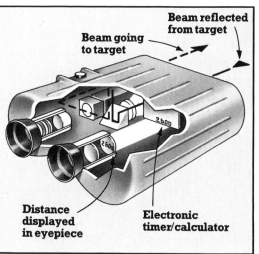

Beam reflected from target

Beam going to target

Distance displayed in eyepiece

Electronic timer/calculator

Laser guidance

Scattered light

Laser beam

Missiles can be guided by laser beam to hit a target. A hidden soldier shines a laser beam onto the target, so that the light hits it and is scattered. The missile has a detector in its nose that picks up and homes in on this scattered light.

Hunter-killer satellites

As laser beams can travel through space easily, they are being considered as space weapons. It may be possible to equip surveillance satellites with lasers so that enemy missiles could be destroyed from space when first spotted.

War "games"

Perhaps the strangest use of lasers is in the full-scale mock battles that armies carry out as practice for possible future war. The commanders want everything to be as realistic as possible, without using dangerous live ammunition. So they use laser "bullets" instead.

Soldiers have optical detectors all over their battledress and safe, low power lasers, like an aiming aid, fixed to their weapons. When a beam hits a detector an alarm is set off, so the soldier knows when he is "dead".

Laser beam

Laser fixed to gun barrel

Optical detectors

Video map displays shots and hits

Each "shot" and "hit" transmits a radio signal to computers which monitor the whole battle. The action is displayed on video maps for the commanders to see, rather like a complicated, real life computer game.

37

Lasers in chemistry

Many uses have been found for lasers in different areas of science, especially chemistry. They are used to detect and identify chemical elements and compounds, and to monitor and start reactions. The largest laser in the world is being used to try and develop cheap, safe, nuclear power.

Analysis by light

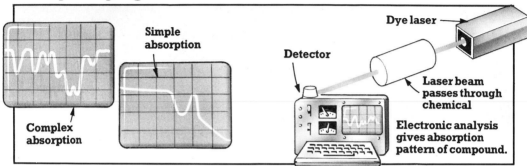

Simple absorption

Complex absorption

Dye laser

Detector

Laser beam passes through chemical

Electronic analysis gives absorption pattern of compound.

Chemists can find out a lot about chemical compounds by studying how they absorb different wavelengths of light. The chemicals in a substance can be identified by looking at the pattern of light absorption.

Some compounds have little absorption, in others the absorption pattern is complex. Analysis by light is called spectroscopy and a tunable dye laser is often used, as it can produce many wavelengths.

Chemical reactions

The energy of a laser beam can cause chemical changes in the substance that absorbs the light. The compound may be broken up into different chemicals and this process can be used to purify compounds. By tuning the laser to a wavelength absorbed by just one of the chemicals, the beam separates only those atoms or molecules, without harming the others.

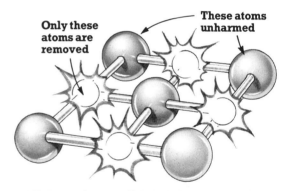

Only these atoms are removed

These atoms unharmed

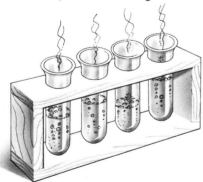

High power lasers can also be used to set off chemical reactions. They do this by breaking up the molecules with an intense flash of light. Once the reaction has begun, it carries on alone.

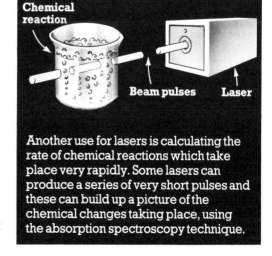

Chemical reaction

Beam pulses

Laser

Another use for lasers is calculating the rate of chemical reactions which take place very rapidly. Some lasers can produce a series of very short pulses and these can build up a picture of the chemical changes taking place, using the absorption spectroscopy technique.

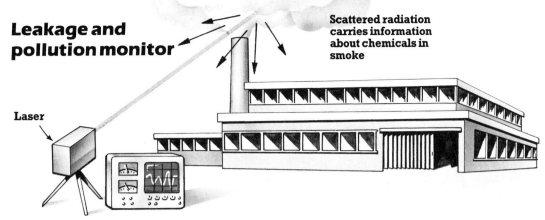

Leakage and pollution monitor

Laser

Scattered radiation carries information about chemicals in smoke

Laser spectroscopy can be helpful in looking for pollution and leaks of dangerous chemicals. This picture shows laser analysis of a plume of smoke from a factory chimney, checking for dangerous levels of poisonous pollutants. Laser detectors are very sensitive and can detect minute amounts of pollutant – levels of less than one part per million. They can run continuously and be connected to an alarm system.

Laser nuclear fusion

The ultimate chemical reaction is changing one element into another. Medieval alchemists tried to turn ordinary metals into gold, but failed. This "transmutation" does take place now, in nuclear reactions. The Sun is such a reactor as it fuses hydrogen into helium, producing energy which reaches us as light and heat. The same process causes the destructive energy of the hydrogen bomb. It requires enormous pressures and vast temperatures.

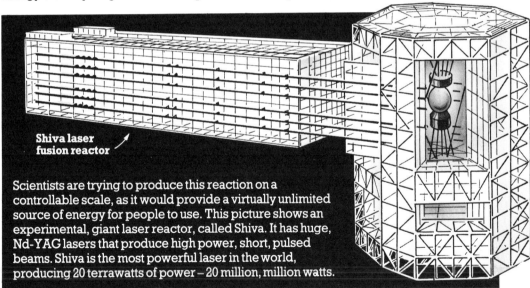

Shiva laser fusion reactor

Scientists are trying to produce this reaction on a controllable scale, as it would provide a virtually unlimited source of energy for people to use. This picture shows an experimental, giant laser reactor, called Shiva. It has huge, Nd-YAG lasers that produce high power, short, pulsed beams. Shiva is the most powerful laser in the world, producing 20 terrawatts of power – 20 million, million watts.

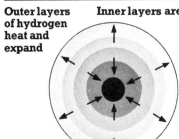

Outer layers of hydrogen heat and expand

Inner layers are compressed

Pellets of hydrogen are bombarded by these pulsed beams. The outer layers heat up very rapidly and expand, the inner layers of hydrogen are compressed. This should lead to nuclear fusion and production of energy. Shiva is just one experiment towards fusion and there is a long way to go before your home will be heated and lit by power from lasers.

39

Computing with lasers

Light travels faster than anything in the universe and scientists are trying to use the speed of laser beams to build faster computers. These two pages explain the research being carried out to apply lasers to the basic workings of the computer. Don't worry if you find this difficult to follow, it is very new research and unlikely to be in use until the next century.

How computers work

Computers are information processors which work by turning all information into a very simple code. This code is made up of just two signals – on and off – which can be written down as 1 and 0. It is called a binary digital code. Within the computer the code is actually produced by electonic switches, called transistors, which are either on or off.

TV screen

Keyboard

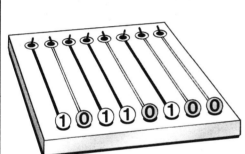

Since their invention almost 40 years ago, transistors have increased in switching speed and at present the fastest takes a nanosecond (thousand millionth of a second) to complete each switching operation. A switch which worked with light, instead of electronically, could be a 1000 times faster, switching every picosecond.

Optical "transistors"

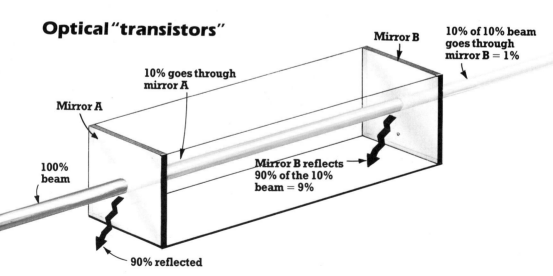

Mirror B

10% of 10% beam goes through mirror B = 1%

10% goes through mirror A

Mirror A

100% beam

Mirror B reflects 90% of the 10% beam = 9%

90% reflected

Experimental versions of optical transistors, called transphasors, have already been developed. They use the principle of interference to do the switching and so need laser light to work.

A transphasor is made of two mirrors with a space called the cavity in between. Both mirrors are partially silvered so that they reflect 90% of the laser beam and let through (transmit) 10% of it, as shown here.

How transphasors work

As laser light is coherent, interference takes place between the light waves going into the cavity through mirror A and those reflected by mirror B. If the two sets of light waves are out of phase, they will cancel each other out (destructive interference). If they are in phase they will reinforce each other (constructive interference). The kind of interference depends upon the distance between the mirrors.

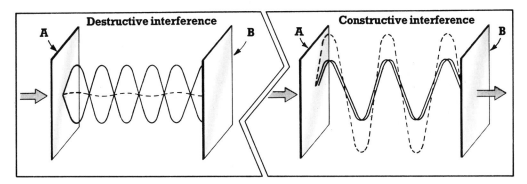

When there is destructive interference in the cavity almost no light gets through mirror B, because the light waves are cancelling each other out. The transphasor is switched off.

When there is constructive interference the light waves build up within the cavity and mirror B lets through a beam almost as bright as the original. The transphasor is switched on.

Optical switching

The next step is to switch the transphasor between on and off. This was done by using the ability of some materials to slow down the passage of light. Making the light travel slower has the same effect as moving the mirrors. Light travels at a constant 300 million m/s in a vacuum and in the air, but various materials, such as water and glass, slow it down. The cavity of the transphasor is filled with a special material which doesn't just slow the light, but slows it according to brightness. The brighter the beam, the slower it goes.

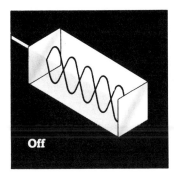

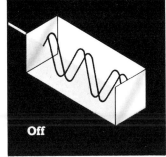

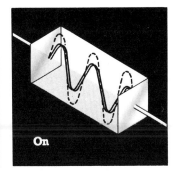

These pictures above show how an optical switching is done. The transphasor is off, as the mirrors are set for destructive interference.

As the brightness of the beam is increased, the material in the cavity slows the light. This changes the interference towards constructive.

If the intensity of the light continues to increase, the point of constructive interference is reached and the transphasor switches on.

Lasers at work

When the laser was first invented about 25 years ago, there were few obvious uses for it. Since then, however, an amazing range of things have been found for it to do. You probably have lots of things at home that were produced with the help of lasers in some way, although it is unlikely to be obvious – clothes, furniture, sunglasses, newspapers, electronic equipment, to name just a few.

Lasers fit into modern, high-tech industry because they are precise, accurate and controllable tools. They are very well suited for use with other new machines like robots and computers. The next four pages show more of the jobs lasers do, or are planned for them.

Road scanner

Beams bounce off road surface

This van scans the road as it travels by bouncing laser beams off the surface. The resulting measurements are analysed by a microprocessor on board, to provide data on the state of the road.

The Daily Laser

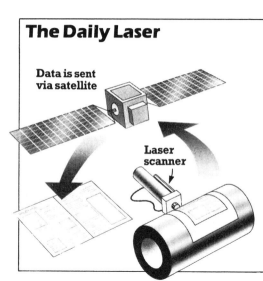

Data is sent via satellite

Laser scanner

The newspaper *USA Today* is a daily which covers the whole of the country. This is only possible using new technology, like lasers and satellites, as the USA is too large for country-wide distribution using ordinary methods. Laser scanners turn the words and pictures of each page into computerized data. This is then sent, via satellite, to newspaper printers all over the country, in a matter of seconds. At the receiving offices lasers are used to reconstruct and print the pages, so a single edition goes out all over the country at the same time.

Laser sight test

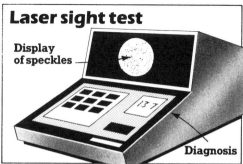

Display of speckles

Diagnosis

This machine uses the speckled coherence of laser light to test eyesight. If you have defective vision the speckles move – up for long sight, down for short sight. The speed shows how bad your eyesight is.

Shuttle docking

Shuttle's cargo bay open

Laser beam

Lasers will help Shuttle recover satellites on repair missions. Reflective pads on the satellite bounce the beam back, giving Shuttle's computers precise measurements so it can steer the craft to the satellite.

Gem security

MN 05735 700

Characters only visible with microscope

This picture shows a magnified view of part of a diamond. The microscopically tiny characters were engraved by laser onto the edge of the gem as an identification code to aid recovery if the diamond is stolen.

Unclogging arteries

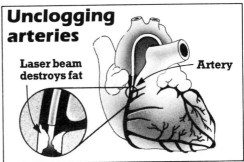

Laser beam destroys fat

Artery

Heart disease is often caused by fatty deposits in arteries of the heart. Tests show that lasers, delivered by optical fibres, could be used to vaporize this fat and unclog arteries.

Gas sniffer

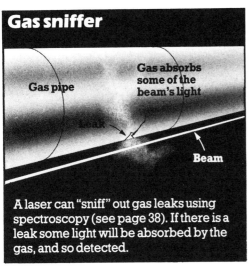

Gas absorbs some of the beam's light

Gas pipe

Beam

A laser can "sniff" out gas leaks using spectroscopy (see page 38). If there is a leak some light will be absorbed by the gas, and so detected.

Laser money

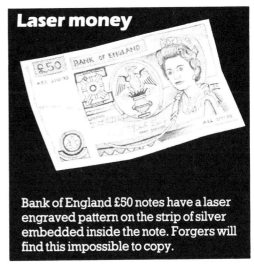

Bank of England £50 notes have a laser engraved pattern on the strip of silver embedded inside the note. Forgers will find this impossible to copy.

Eye drill

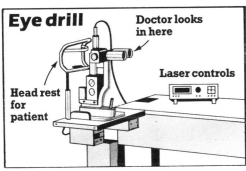

Doctor looks in here

Laser controls

Head rest for patient

Some eye problems are caused by a build up of pressure inside the eyeball. This can be treated by drilling tiny holes, with a laser, in the eye's outer surface to release the tension.

Flight display

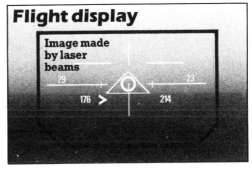

Image made by laser beams

This picture shows how lasers project an image of the controls of an aircraft onto the windscreen so that the pilot does not have to look down at them. It is called a Head Up Display (H.U.D.).

Fingerprint scanner

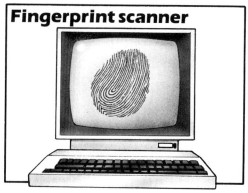

Everyone has unique fingerprints made up of whorls and ridges. They can be scanned by laser beam and the data stored on computer. This can be used by police, or even to enable your fingers to act as the key for a laser lock.

Laser wine taster

The taste of a wine depends upon the size of clumps of protein molecules that form within it – the smaller the clumps the tastier the wine. The quality of the wine can be measured by laser as the larger clumps scatter more light than the smaller ones.

Diamond holes

Impurity is vaporized by laser beam

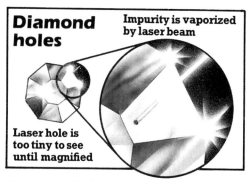

Laser hole is too tiny to see until magnified

Diamond is the hardest known substance but it can be drilled by laser. Faults such as spots of carbon can be removed by drilling a tiny, invisible hole in the gem and vaporizing the black flecks.

Batting monitor

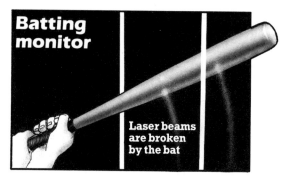

Laser beams are broken by the bat

Lasers are even used to time baseball batters' reactions and to monitor their batting power, speed and style. Two lasers make the measurements when the batter swings the bat through the beams.

Treating tumours

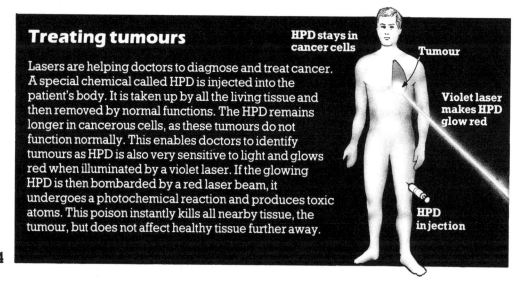

HPD stays in cancer cells

Tumour

Violet laser makes HPD glow red

HPD injection

Lasers are helping doctors to diagnose and treat cancer. A special chemical called HPD is injected into the patient's body. It is taken up by all the living tissue and then removed by normal functions. The HPD remains longer in cancerous cells, as these tumours do not function normally. This enables doctors to identify tumours as HPD is also very sensitive to light and glows red when illuminated by a violet laser. If the glowing HPD is then bombarded by a red laser beam, it undergoes a photochemical reaction and produces toxic atoms. This poison instantly kills all nearby tissue, the tumour, but does not affect healthy tissue further away.

Laser gun TV

A colour TV picture is made up of hundreds of horizontal lines formed from tiny glowing dots. In present TVs the spots are made by three electron guns; one each for red, blue and green. This system can only produce a picture on a special phosphor covered surface. In a new system lasers produce the red, green and blue beams which are combined to make the moving picture. The beams and spot are moved by a series of electronically controlled mirrors to create a picture. The image is much clearer than conventional TV and can be projected onto any surface.

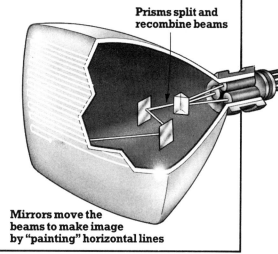

Prisms split and recombine beams

Mirrors move the beams to make image by "painting" horizontal lines

Light music

Laser beams

Photodetectors sends signals to synthesizer

This harp has laser beam "strings" which are played by passing your hand through the beams. The broken beams send signals to an electronic music synthesizer, which produces the notes.

Slow release medicine

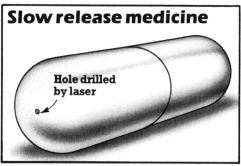

Hole drilled by laser

Many diseases need to be treated by an even level of drugs in the blood. This capsule has a tiny laser-drilled hole in its shell which releases a steady, constant dose of medicine.

Laser bug

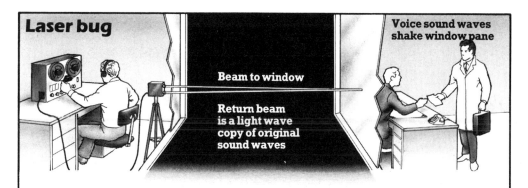

Voice sound waves shake window pane

Beam to window

Return beam is a light wave copy of original sound waves

A laser beam can be used to eavesdrop on a conversation, by bouncing the beam off the window of a room where people are talking. Their voices make tiny vibrations in the window pane. These would be picked up by the laser beam and carried back to a detector which turns the vibrations back into sounds.

Laser words

Argon: An inert gas used for filling fluorescent lamps and light bulbs. When excited, it produces laser action at green, blue and ultra-violet wavelengths.

Carbon dioxide: A gas produced by the burning of carbon compounds in air. When suitably excited by an electric current, it produces laser action as a long infra-red wavelength. When mixed with nitrogen and helium the laser output is increased.

Coherent: Describes electromagnetic radiation that has a single phase. The waves are all in step with one another, that is their peaks and troughs coincide with each other. Lasers produce coherent light but sources such as light bulbs and fluorescent tubes do not.

Electromagnetic radiation: Waves of energy with wavelengths varying from less than a million millionth of a metre to more than ten thousand metres and including all kinds of light, radio waves and X-rays. All electromagnetic radiation travels at 300 million metres per second in air.

Excitation: The process of increasing the energy of atoms or molecules into higher energy states. In lasers, this can be done, for example, by illuminating solids with light or by passing an electric current through gases.

Focus: The spot to which rays of light are converged by lenses or mirrors. With laser light, the size of the focused spot depends on the wavelength of the laser. Visible and near infra-red laser beams can be focused to about 2 or 3 micrometres, while carbon dioxide lasers are limited to about 50 micrometres.

Frequency: The number of complete waves produced in a second by a source. For electromagnetic waves, the frequency is obtained by dividing the velocity by the wavelength.

Fusion: A nuclear reaction in which one or more light elements join together to make a heavier one. In the Sun, hydrogen is being continuously fused into helium. This reaction, which also takes place in the hydrogen bomb, releases a large amount of energy. It can only take place at very high temperatures and intense pressure.

Helium neon: Two inert gases which, when mixed together and excited electrically, produce laser action. Helium neon lasers produce both visible and infra-red light but are used mostly as simple, comparatively cheap, red laser sources for alignment, etc.

Hologram: A three-dimensional recording of an image on photographic film or a photographic plate, using a laser light source.

Interference: Effect caused when two or more waves overlap. If peaks from two equal waves coincide, a bigger wave is produced (constructive interference) but when a peak coincides with a trough there is cancellation and the wave disappears (destructive interference).

Interference pattern (interferogram): The pattern produced by interfering waves. For two equal waves the pattern will vary from double size peaks to zero.

Interferometer: An instrument designed to produce interference effects. Interferometers can be used to measure the wavelength of light or, when used with a particular wavelength, to measure small distances very accurately.

Laser: The acronym (first letter of each word) of the phrase which describes the working of the device – Light Amplification by Stimulated Emission of Radiation.

Lens: A device, usually made of glass or quartz, for converging (focusing) or diverging a beam of light. Convex lenses converge and concave lenses diverge light.

Light: Historically used to describe electromagnetic radiation that is visible to the eye. Now it includes ultra-violet and infra-red wavelengths. Light that can be seen is called visible light.

Nd-glass, Nd-YAG: Neodymium has a set of energy levels suitable for laser action. Neodymium is put into a suitable material which transmits the laser light. YAG (yttrium aluminium garnet) and glass are the most common host materials.

Optical fibre: A very thin strand of glass or plastic which can carry light. Glass fibres are quite flexible and will transmit an infra-red laser signal over more than 100 kilometres.

Prism: A triangular shaped block, normally of glass or quartz for visible light, which bends (refracts) different colours at different angles. When white light falls on a prism it is separated into a spectrum.

Ruby: A form of aluminium oxide containing chromium. Chromium has a set of energy levels suitable for laser action.

Spectroscopy: The analysis of solid liquids and gases by studying their absorption and transmission of electromagnetic radiation of different wavelengths. Tunable lasers are particularly useful for this type of analysis.

Spectrum: Normally used to describe the range of colours that make up visible light. It is also often used to describe the whole range of electromagnetic radiation, when it is called the electromagnetic spectrum.

Transphasor: A term used to describe the optical equivalent of a transistor. In a computer, the electrical output of a transistor can be switched by an electrical pulse. In an optical computer, the light output of a transphasor can be switched by a pulse of light.

Wavelength: The distance between successive peaks of a wave. For example, green light has a wavelength of 500 nanometres.

White light: Light that is made up of all the visible wavelengths and appears white to the human eye.

Abbreviations

Ar	argon
Au	gold
CO	carbon monoxide
CO_2	carbon dioxide
Cu	copper
CW	continuous wave
HAZ	heat affected zone
HBr	hydrogen bromide
HCN	hydrogen cyanide
HeCd	helium cadmium
HeNe	helium neon
HF	hydrogen fluoride
I-R	infra-red
Kr	krypton
KrF	krypton fluoride
m/s	metres per second
N_2	nitrogen
Nd-glass	neodymium in glass
Nd-YAG	neodymium-yag
U-V	ultra-violet
YAG	yttrium aluminium garnet

Measurements

micrometre	millionth of a metre
nanometre	thousand millionth of a metre
millisecond	thousandth of a second
microsecond	millionth of a second
nanosecond	thousandth millionth of a second
picosecond	million millionth of a second
kilowatt	thousand watts
megawatt	million watts
gigawatt	thousand million watts
terrawatt	million million watts

Going further

Here are some of the galleries that have permanent exhibitions of holograms. You may find that your local museum or art gallery has visiting displays and there may even be shops selling small holograms and holographic jewellery.

Light Fantastic Gallery of Holography
48 South Row
The Market
Covent Garden
London WC2

National Museum of Film, Photography
    and Television
Bradford
West Yorkshire

Northern Light Fantastic
Edinburgh Wax Museum
142 High Street
Edinburgh

ZAP
45 Barlow Moor Road
Didsbury
Manchester

Holos Gallery
1792 Haight Street
San Francisco

Museum of Holography
11 Mercer Street
New York

Index

The name Usborne and the device are
Trade Marks of Usborne Publishing Ltd.

PRINTED IN BELGIUM